DODGE
CHALLENGER
SRT HELLCAT

BY EMILY ROSE OACHS

BELLWETHER MEDIA • MINNEAPOLIS, MN

™

Are you ready to take it to the extreme?
Torque books thrust you into the action-packed world
of sports, vehicles, mystery, and adventure. These books
may include dirt, smoke, fire, and dangerous stunts.
WARNING: read at your own risk.

This edition first published in 2017 by Bellwether Media, Inc.

No part of this publication may be reproduced in whole or in part without written permission of the publisher.
For information regarding permission, write to Bellwether Media, Inc., Attention: Permissions Department,
5357 Penn Avenue South, Minneapolis, MN 55419.

Library of Congress Cataloging-in-Publication Data

Names: Oachs, Emily Rose, author.
Title: Dodge Challenger SRT Hellcat / by Emily Rose Oachs.
Other titles: Car Crazy (Minneapolis, Minn.)
Description: Minneapolis, MN : Bellwether Media, Inc., 2017. | Series:
   Torque: Car Crazy | Audience: Ages 7-12. | Includes bibliographical
   references and index.
Identifiers: LCCN 2016035473 (print) | LCCN 2016036394 (ebook) | ISBN
   9781626175778 (hardcover : alk. paper) | ISBN 9781681033068 (ebook)
Subjects: LCSH: Challenger automobile–Juvenile literature.
Classification: LCC TL215.C44 O23 2017 (print) | LCC TL215.C44 (ebook) | DDC
   629.222/2–dc23
LC record available at https://lccn.loc.gov/2016035473

Editor: Betsy Rathburn   Designer: Brittany McIntosh

Printed in the United States of America, North Mankato, MN.

TABLE OF CONTENTS

TOO POWERFUL TO BE REAL?

A Dodge Challenger SRT Hellcat crawls onto an empty track. A crowd of people looks on. They have heard about this new Challenger **model**. But it sounds too powerful to be real. They want to see it for themselves.

Without warning, the driver presses the pedal to the floor. The car zooms down the **straightaway**. It runs the quarter-mile in less than 11 seconds!

The driver finishes the lap. As the car stops, the crowd claps and cheers. The Challenger SRT Hellcat did not let them down!

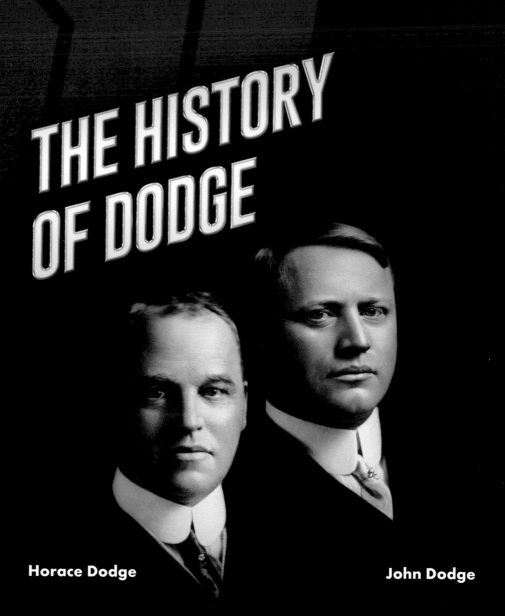

THE HISTORY OF DODGE

Horace Dodge

John Dodge

Horace and John Dodge liked to build bicycles during the late 1800s. In 1900, these brothers moved on to automobiles. They started a **machine shop** in Detroit, Michigan. There, they built parts for carmakers like Oldsmobile and Ford.

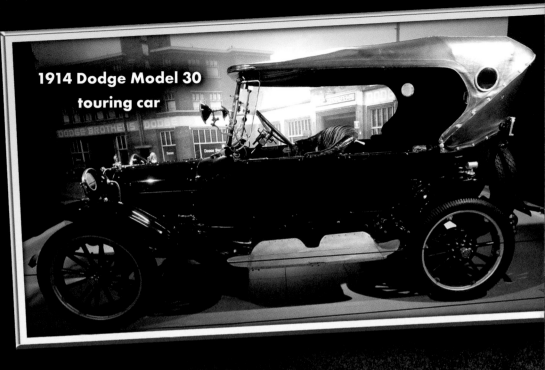

1914 Dodge Model 30 touring car

BOOMING BUSINESS
THE DODGE BROTHERS BUILT ONLY 249 CARS IN 1914. BUT THEY MADE MORE THAN 45,000 THE FOLLOWING YEAR!

1970 Dodge Challenger R/T

By 1915, Dodge was among the largest carmakers in the country. However, both brothers passed away in 1920. In 1928, Dodge was purchased by the Chrysler Company.

Chrysler introduced the Dodge Challenger in 1969. Since then, the company has added many new cars to the Dodge lineup. Drivers trust Dodge to sell good cars at a fair price.

DODGE CHALLENGER SRT HELLCAT

Dodge introduced the Challenger SRT Hellcat in 2014. It was the newest addition to the famous Challenger line of **muscle cars**.

The Challenger SRT Hellcat wows car lovers with its powerful engine and **acceleration**. It takes just 3.6 seconds to reach 60 miles (97 kilometers) per hour!

2015 Dodge Challenger
SRT Hellcat

2016 Dodge Challenger
SRT Hellcat

TECHNOLOGY AND GEAR

At the heart of the Challenger SRT Hellcat is its **V8 engine**. This engine makes the Hellcat one of the fastest muscle cars on the road. A **supercharger** pumps more air into the engine. This gives it an added power boost.

Twin hood **air extractors** help cool the engine. They also make the car more **aerodynamic**.

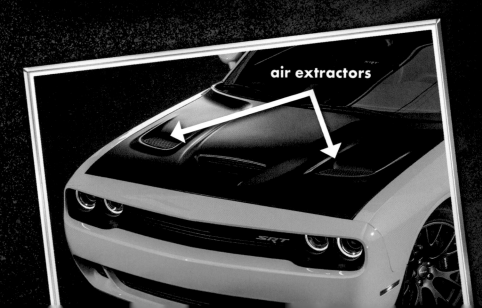

air extractors

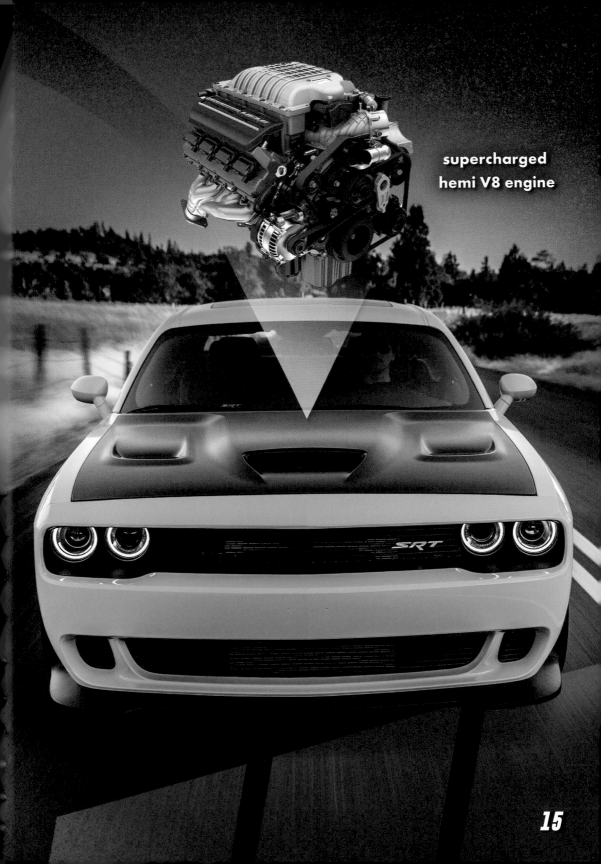

supercharged
hemi V8 engine

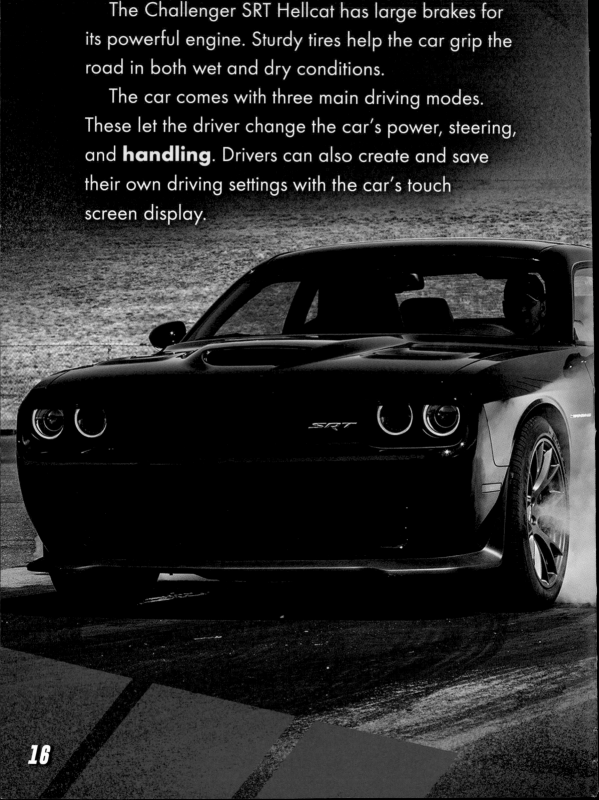

The Challenger SRT Hellcat has large brakes for its powerful engine. Sturdy tires help the car grip the road in both wet and dry conditions.

The car comes with three main driving modes. These let the driver change the car's power, steering, and **handling**. Drivers can also create and save their own driving settings with the car's touch screen display.

touch screen display

UNLOCKING POWER

HELLCAT OWNERS RECEIVE TWO DIFFERENT CAR KEYS. WITH THE RED KEY, OWNERS DRIVE WITH THE ENGINE'S FULL POWER. THE BLACK KEY LIMITS DRIVERS TO 500 HORSEPOWER (373 KILOWATTS).

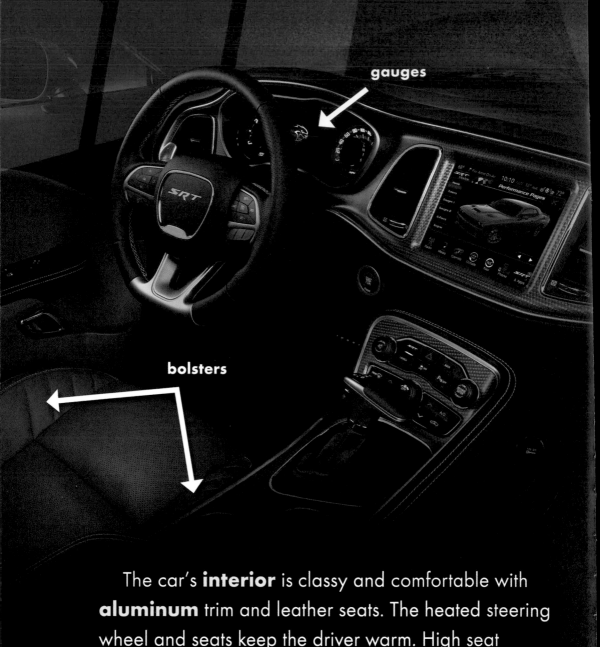

gauges

bolsters

The car's **interior** is classy and comfortable with **aluminum** trim and leather seats. The heated steering wheel and seats keep the driver warm. High seat **bolsters** give the Hellcat a race car feel.

Behind the wheel are red-rimmed **gauges**. The touch screen display sits on the dashboard. These features allow the driver to check the car's performance.

2016 DODGE CHALLENGER SRT HELLCAT SPECIFICATIONS

CAR STYLE	COUPE
ENGINE	6.2L SUPERCHARGED HEMI V8
TOP SPEED	199 MILES (320 KILOMETERS) PER HOUR
0 - 60 TIME	3.6 SECONDS
HORSEPOWER	707 HP (527 KILOWATTS) @ 6,000 RPM
CURB WEIGHT	4,469 POUNDS (2,027 KILOGRAMS)
WIDTH	75.7 INCHES (192 CENTIMETERS)
LENGTH	197.2 INCHES (501 CENTIMETERS)
HEIGHT	57.1 INCHES (145 CENTIMETERS)
WHEEL SIZE	20 INCHES (51 CENTIMETERS)
COST	STARTS AT $64,195

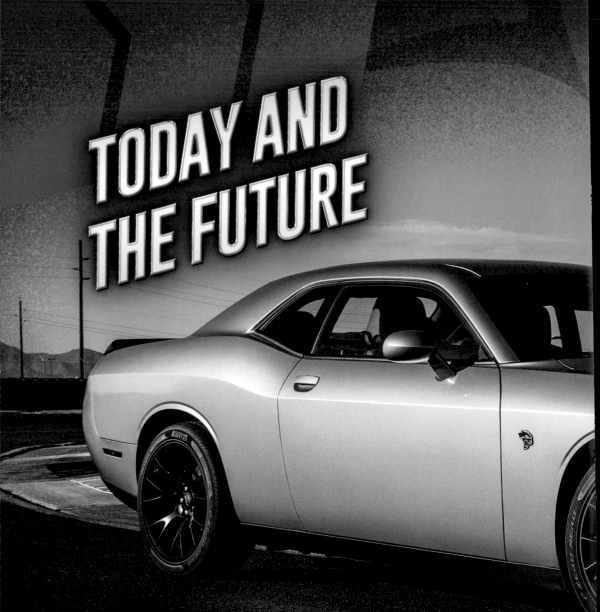

TODAY AND THE FUTURE

The Hellcat was an instant success. There were thousands of orders before it was released.

The car's outstanding power and **vintage** style still appeal to many fans today. Drivers also love how well the car moves on both the highway and the track. The Challenger SRT Hellcat has proven that it will be the muscle car to beat for years to come!

HOW TO SPOT A DODGE CHALLENGER SRT HELLCAT

1970S-INSPIRED TAILLIGHTS   **SPOILER**   **AIR EXTRACTORS**

GOING, GOING, GONE!

MANY CAR LOVERS WANTED THE NEW CHALLENGER SRT HELLCAT FOR THEMSELVES. DEALERS SOLD OUT IN LESS THAN A YEAR OF ITS RELEASE!

GLOSSARY

acceleration—an increase in speed

aerodynamic—having a shape that can move through the air quickly

air extractors—vents that draw cooler air toward the engine

aluminum—a strong, lightweight metal

bolsters—cushions on either side of a seat

gauges—devices that measure or track something

handling—how a car performs around turns

interior—the inside of a car

machine shop—a company that builds or fixes machine parts made of metal or hard plastic

model—a specific kind of car

muscle cars—high-performance sports cars with strong engines

straightaway—the straight part of a track

supercharger—a part that increases an engine's power

V8 engine—an engine with 8 cylinders arranged in the shape of a "V"

vintage—classic or from an earlier time

TO LEARN MORE

AT THE LIBRARY

Gifford, Clive. *Car Crazy*. New York, N.Y.: D.K. Publishing, 2012.

Gray, Leon. *Fast and Cool Cars*. New York, N.Y.: DK, Penguin Random House, 2015.

Hamilton, John. *Muscle Cars*. Minneapolis, Minn.: ABDO Pub., 2013.

ON THE WEB

Learning more about the Dodge Challenger SRT Hellcat is as easy as 1, 2, 3.

1. Go to www.factsurfer.com.

2. Enter "Dodge Challenger SRT Hellcat" into the search box.

3. Click the "Surf" button and you will see a list of related web sites.

With factsurfer.com, finding more information is just a click away.

INDEX

The images in this book are reproduced through the courtesy of: Hunter J.G. Frim Photography, front cover; Chrysler, pp. 4-5, 6-7, 8, 9, 13, 14, 15 (top, bottom), 16, 17 (top, bottom), 18, 19, 20-21, 21 (top left, top center, top right); Sicnag/ Flickr, pp. 10-11; Steve Lagreca, p. 12.